THIRD GRADE WEDDING BELLS?

THIRD GRADE WEDDING BELLS?

by COLLEEN
O'SHAUGHNESSY
McKENNA

illustrated by
STEPHANIE ROTH

Ms. Tingle
+
Mr. Wilson

Holiday House / New York

This book is dedicated to the
following happy couples:
Collette and Kirk Parker
Dana and Jeff McKenna
Laura and Paul Miller
C. O. M.

To two great teachers, Jamie Berry and Angel
Hutchins. Thanks for making a difference.

S. R.

Text copyright © 2006 by Colleen O'Shaughnessy McKenna
Illustrations copyright © 2006 by Stephanie Roth
All Rights Reserved
Printed in the United States of America
www.holidayhouse.com
First Edition
2   4   6   8   10   9   7   5   3   1

Library of Congress Cataloging-in-Publication Data

McKenna, Colleen O'Shaughnessy.
    Third grade wedding bells? / by Colleen O'Shaughnessy McKenna ;
illustrated by Stephanie Roth.—1st ed.
        p. cm.
    Summary: Third grade is a big disappointment for Gordie who dreads
having to kiss Lucy in the class play and despairs that his favorite teacher,
Ms. Tingle, may be getting married.
    ISBN: 0-8234-1943-6
    [1. Schools—Fiction.   2. Teachers—Fiction.   3. Theater—Fiction.]
I. Roth, Stephanie, ill.   II. Title.

PZ7.M1983Tk 2006
[Fic]—dc22   2005050262

    ISBN-13: 978-0-8234-1943-2
    ISBN-10: 0-8234-1943-6

Chapter 1

"Here's my snowman, Ms. Tingle. Can you hang him next to Lamont's polar bear?" asked Gordie.

"Of course." Ms. Tingle taped the snowman on the windowpane above the fish tank. The snowman's head was a little small, but his Pittsburgh Steeler cap looked great.

"Here's my penguin," announced Lucy Diaz. "When everyone finishes his or her polar pet, can we try out for the holiday play?"

"Of course," said Ms. Tingle. "It's the first play I've ever written."

"It's a great play." Lucy smiled at Gordie.

"And I'm already ready. I want to be Snow White."

"So do I," said Leslie. "Snow White has the most lines in the whole play."

"Sixty-two lines," said Lucy. "Which is why I should be Snow White. I have the best memory in the whole third grade. Even my mother thinks so."

"I'm in the highest reading group, just like you," said Leslie.

"Which part would you like, Gordie?" asked Ms. Tingle.

"He should be happy with a very small part," said Lucy. "He ruined the second grade play."

"I did not." The only thing Gordie didn't like about third grade was having Lucy in his class. He even had to share a locker with her.

"We were all candy canes. But then Gordie ran off the stage," explained Lucy.

"I forgot my lines," said Gordie.

"I'm sure you'll do a good job this year," said Ms. Tingle.

"Okay, class. Let's finish up the art project and then get out your scripts for the holiday play."

Lucy followed Gordie back to their seats. "I just have to be Snow White. It's the most important role."

Gordie slumped into his seat. "Nobody knows who the star will be, Lucy. Maybe Leslie will be Snow White."

"Leslie can be Cinderella. She has only forty-three lines." Lucy pushed back her thick black hair. "You could be an elf. The elves just stand around."

Gordie shook his head. "I don't want to wear tights. Maybe I could be an elf that wears blue jeans."

"All elves wear tights," said Lucy. "Santa makes them wear tights so they can run faster and snow won't stick to them."

Lamont leaned over and knocked on Gordie's desk. "I'm going to try out for Santa, ho, ho, ho."

Lucy laughed. "Trust me, you do not look like Santa Claus, Lamont."

"Trust me, Lucy, you are no Snow White. You are more of a Snow Flake." Lamont and Gordie high-fived each other.

Lucy studied her script. "Gordie, maybe you could be Rudolph. He has only two lines. Lines like, 'My nose is red.' And, 'I will lead the sleigh.' Even *you* can handle that."

"Ha, ha," said Gordie. "You are so not funny, Lucy. I could memorize a hundred lines if I wanted to learn them."

Lamont and Lucy both laughed.

Lamont picked up his script. "Hey, forget Rudolph, Gordie. You should try out for the part of the prince. He only comes onstage at the end of the play. That's the good news. The bad news is that you'd have to kiss Snow White."

Gordie and Lucy flew out of their seats.

"No way," said Gordie. If he had to kiss Lucy Diaz, he wouldn't run off the stage, he'd jump off the stage.

"No way, double way," added Lucy. "You are not going to mess up this play, Gordie."

"I don't even want to *be* in the play," muttered Gordie. He wished he could be in the audience, or in charge of opening the curtains.

"Good," said Lucy. She sat back down and flipped her hair over her shoulders. "Because you were the worst candy cane of all last year. Even my mother said so."

"Get out your scripts, class. Time for auditions," called out Ms. Tingle.

"Lamont, tell me the truth about something," Gordie said.

Lamont nodded. "Best friends always tell the truth."

"Lucy said I was the worst candy cane in the second grade play."

"Yeah, you were, boy." Lamont laughed. "You just disappeared."

Gordie clenched his teeth. Lamont was telling too much truth.

"Boys, sit down now," said Ms. Tingle. "Turn to page two in the script."

Gordie flipped through his script. He had waited his whole life to have Ms. Tingle as his teacher. He would help make her play the best, no matter how many lines he had to memorize.

Chapter 2

Five kids had tried out for the play before it was time to line up for lunch.

Lucy stood up and waved her script in the air. "Can I try out for Snow White now? I make straight As. I have black hair, and I can even sing if you want me to."

Gordie and Lamont looked at each other and laughed.

"After lunch, Lucy," said Ms. Tingle. "Time to line up, children."

Lamont stood up and stretched. "Watch out for those poisoned apples, Lucy."

"Very funny, Lamont," said Lucy. But

she grinned at him. "Just make sure Gordie is your elf and not my prince."

"I can be whatever I want, Lucy," said Gordie.

"Hey, Gordie." Lamont shook Gordie's arm. "What are you giving Ms. Tingle for Christmas?"

"I'm not sure," said Gordie.

"I'm giving her this." Lamont reached into his pocket and handed Gordie a ring. It was a large ring with a dog's head carved out of something hard. The dog looked like he was choking on something.

"I found it at my granny's church sale. The lady wanted five bucks for it, but I offered her thirty-five cents and she took it."

"Ms. Tingle will like it, Lamont." Gordie gave the ring back. Maybe Ms. Tingle could wear it when she was outside by herself, pulling weeds, or when she was asleep, so no one would see it.

Lamont slid the ring back into his pocket.

"Boy, I'm hungry," said Gordie. "The hall smells like pizza today. I hope it's pepperoni."

Lucy turned around. "I'm allergic to pepperoni."

"I'm allergic to you," added Mikey. His face flashed bright red because everyone knew he liked Lucy. Since Lucy was bossy and bragged all the time, Gordie wasn't sure why anyone liked her.

"After recess Ms. Tingle will give everyone a part for the holiday play," said Lamont.

Gordie sighed. He hoped he got the smallest part. He tried not to think about it as he followed Lamont into the cafeteria.

Gordie picked up a tray from the stack and turned, right into Mr. Wilson, the new computer teacher.

"Slow down, sonny," said Mr. Wilson. He reached over and grabbed some napkins.

As soon as Mr. Wilson left, Lamont bumped his tray into Gordie's back. "Sorry, sonny."

Gordie laughed as he watched Mr. Wilson walk over to Ms. Tingle and hand her a small white bag.

"What's in the bag?" asked Lamont.

Lucy turned around. "Probably a diamond ring, sonny boy."

Gordie knew Ms. Tingle would never like someone like Mr. Wilson. Besides, she was too busy being their teacher to have a boyfriend.

Gordie pushed his tray along, taking an apple and watching Ms. Tingle pull a large doughnut out of the white bag.

Gordie and Lamont passed Lucy and headed for the tables.

Lucy said, "I have a big, gigantic secret."

"Who cares," muttered Lamont. "Come on, Gordie."

Lucy hurried to catch up. "It's the best secret of my life. Did you know that Mr. Wilson calls Ms. Tingle 'Rebecca'? That's her real name."

Rebecca? Gordie stopped so fast that Lamont plowed into the back of him. Lamont's apple flew off his tray and rolled across the cafeteria floor like a bowling ball.

"Wild apple on the loose!" called out Lamont.

Lucy set her tray down and sat down. "Mr. Wilson patted Ms. Tingle's hand and said, 'I don't know what I'd do without you, Rebecca.'"

"*What?*" asked Gordie. He didn't even know Ms. Tingle had a first name.

"Rebecca, Rebecca, Rebecca," chanted Lucy.

"Her name is Ms. Tingle, Lucy." Gordie felt a little funny that Lucy knew more about Ms. Tingle than he did. "Even the principal calls her Ms. Tingle."

Lamont nodded, his mouth full of pizza. "The whole world calls her Ms. Tingle."

Lucy pointed a carrot stick at Gordie. "You boys are so dumb. You probably think Ms. Tingle's very own mother called her 'Ms. Tingle' when she was a baby. 'Goo, goo, baby, Ms. Tingle.'"

Lamont laughed so hard he started choking.

Gordie had never even thought of Ms. Tingle as having a mother or being a baby. He'd just thought of her waiting inside room nine to be his teacher.

"Your big secret isn't very good," said Gordie.

"There's lots more to my secret," said Lucy.

"Keep your secret a secret, Lucy. I don't care." Lamont took a big bite of his pizza.

Lucy smiled a mean smile. "Eat your pizza, then. I'll keep my secret all to myself."

"What's the secret?" Gordie asked.

Lucy took a big bite and chewed for a very long time.

Gordie elbowed her. "Tell us, Lucy."

Lucy swallowed and took a drink of milk. "I'm not supposed to talk with my mouth full." She took another big bite and chewed some more. Finally she put the pizza down. "The big secret is that Ms.

Tingle and Mr. Wilson like each other. He gives her presents."

"Big deal," said Gordie. "He gave her a doughnut."

"There's another part to the secret." Lucy chewed and chewed.

Lamont thumped down his milk carton. "Come on, Lucy. Tell us."

Lucy stopped chewing. "Okay. I saw Ms. Tingle out on a date with Mr. Wilson. They were in the dark part of a restaurant. There was a red candle on their table. He even wiped spaghetti sauce off her face, which means they are in love and will probably get married."

Gordie stood up so fast his tray spilled onto the floor. "Married?"

Lucy nodded. "And I heard Mr. Wilson telling the gym teacher that he is moving back to Ohio in January to teach high school in Toledo."

Gordie's stomach flipped. If Mr. Wilson married Ms. Tingle, he'd take her to Ohio, too.

Chapter 3

After lunch Gordie kicked a stone around the playground. "Lucy thinks she knows everything about Ms. Tingle."

Lamont shoved his hands into his pockets. "I bet she made the whole thing up."

Gordie looked at the school doors where Ms. Tingle was talking to the second grade teacher, Ms. Alexander. Ms. Tingle didn't look a bit in love.

When room nine came in from lunch, Gordie noticed the white bakery bag on Ms. Tingle's desk. Good, he thought. Ms.

Tingle didn't eat the doughnut. She was probably going to give it back to Mr. Wilson and tell him to eat it himself.

"Take your seats, class," said Ms. Tingle. "Let's get back to the auditions before it's time for gym."

Gordie slid into his seat and got out his script.

Lamont leaned over and knocked on Gordie's desk. "Showtime, buddy."

Lucy twisted around in her seat. "Oh, I forgot one last part of the secret."

"Is everyone ready?" asked Ms. Tingle. "Who wants to go first?"

Lucy spun around so fast she almost fell out of her seat. "I do. I do, Ms. Tingle. I don't even need a script because I know all of Snow White's lines. I know everyone's lines."

"Okay, Lucy. Come up front. Lamont, please read for Santa; Mikey, read for Doc; and Leslie, why don't you read for the evil queen who gives Snow White the apple?"

Lucy reached into her desk and pulled out an apple. "I saved my apple from lunch for a prop."

Gordie couldn't help laughing during their audition. All four of them were really good, even Lucy.

Ms. Tingle kept jotting things down on her clipboard. She looked like a real director.

"Gordie?"

Ms. Tingle was standing by his desk with her clipboard.

"I asked if you'd read for the prince."

Gordie shook his head. "I want to be Rudolph."

"Could you at least read for the prince? You'll have a chance to read for Rudolph, too."

"He should be Rudolph," said Lucy. "Or elf number three. He only has three lines."

"I'll be an elf if I don't have to wear tights," said Gordie.

"All elves wear tights," said Lucy.

"Okay, first read for the prince, Gordie, and then turn to page six and read for elf three," said Ms. Tingle. "Then go to page eight for Rudolph."

Gordie went up front and read his lines. Leslie was trying out for Snow White now. She was really good, but Lucy was better.

Thirty minutes later Ms. Tingle set her clipboard on her desk and clapped. "Thank you all so much. You all did a wonderful job. I know exactly who will be right for each part."

"Am I Snow White?" asked Lucy. "My mom has already started making me my costume."

"I'll post the cast list on the door after school. You can read it as soon as you get to school tomorrow." Ms. Tingle announced, "Time for gym. Let's line up. We'll have a snack when we come back to the room."

Ms. Tingle had her hand on the door when Mr. Wilson walked in without knocking. Even the principal knocked.

"Sorry to interrupt, Reb . . . I mean, Ms. Tingle."

Lucy turned around and raised her eyebrows at Gordie.

Mr. Wilson held his hand in front of his mouth and started whispering to Ms. Tingle. Everyone in room nine knew that Ms. Tingle didn't like whispering in front of other people.

But Ms. Tingle started whispering back.

Gordie put his head down on his desk.

Chapter

4

Three hours later Gordie got off the school bus. His dog, Scratch, raced down the street to meet him. Gordie was so worried about Lucy's secret that he didn't even feel like playing with him.

"I'll play with you later, Scratch," promised Gordie.

"What's up with you?" asked his brother, Doug. He took off his baseball cap and swatted Gordie on the back with it. Getting swatted by Doug was almost like getting a hug from Mom.

"Our class is having a holiday play." Gordie headed up the driveway. "I don't want to be in it, but Ms. Tingle wrote it herself."

Doug laughed. "I hope you aren't going to be a candy cane. Man, you bolted from the stage last year."

Gordie stopped. "I didn't bolt. I walked."

Doug jabbed Gordie on the arm. "You flew off the stage, man. Then that crazy girl, Lucy, started singing about how candy canes like to tap dance and play the piano."

"Lucy is nuts. In fact, she made up all these lies about Ms. Tingle going on a date with Mr. Wilson." Gordie waited for Doug to say that Lucy was a liar.

But Doug nodded and said, "Maybe it's true. Lumpy said he saw Mr. Wilson and Ms. Tingle at the Tomato Patch restaurant."

"Lumpy saw them?"

Gordie raced up the driveway and sat on the bottom step outside the kitchen door. Doug came up behind him and dashed inside.

"Hey, Mom. We're home. I'm starving," said Doug.

All Gordie could think about was Ms. Tingle and Mr. Wilson eating dinner together and talking about getting married.

Scratch walked over, sat down, and put his head on Gordie's knee.

"You're lucky you get to be a dog," said Gordie. "Dogs don't wear tights or have to worry about people getting married and moving to Ohio."

Scratch thumped his left back leg and moaned.

Mom walked out of the kitchen and sat next to Gordie. "Come on in and have your snack, honey."

"I'm not hungry, Mom."

"Not even for Rice Krispies Treats?"

Just then the phone rang, and Doug stuck his head outside. "Hey, Shrimp. Phone for you."

Gordie scrambled to his feet and went inside. He didn't get phone calls unless it was his birthday.

Doug wiggled his eyebrows up and down as he handed Gordie the phone. "It's a girl," he whispered.

A girl? Gordie swallowed.

"Hello?"

"Gordie, this is Lucy."

"Lucy who?"

Gordie yanked the phone away from his ear as Lucy screamed, *"Diaz! How many Lucys do you know?"*

"What do you want?" Gordie turned his back on Doug so he wouldn't have to see Doug kissing his own hand and saying, "Oh, my sweet little Gordie."

"I have another secret."

Gordie felt like hanging up. He was tired of Lucy's secrets. "So, what is it?"

"Well, my mom drove me back to school because I left my jacket in our locker and it cost over a hundred dollars. Anyway, I saw Ms. Tingle taping the cast list on the door." Lucy laughed. "Actually Mr. Wilson was taping it up; Ms. Tingle just handed him the little pieces of tape. They were laughing a lot."

Gordie squeezed the phone handle so tightly he was afraid it might break. Why wasn't Mr. Wilson in the computer room where he belonged?

"Guess what?" said Lucy.

Gordie could barely speak. "What?"

"I got the part of Snow White."

Gordie waited for the rest of the news.

Lucy would make a good Snow White. "You already know all the lines."

"Right." Gordie could hear Lucy sigh. "But that's not the problem."

"What?"

Lucy sighed again. It was louder this time. "Ms. Tingle chose you to be my prince."

"But I want to be elf three. Or Rudolph."

"Mikey is elf three," said Lucy. "Just make sure you don't run off the stage before you kiss me, or I'll have to stay asleep forever."

Gordie hung up the phone without saying good-bye. He didn't want Ms. Tingle to move to Toledo, he didn't want to be a prince, and he really didn't want to kiss Lucy Diaz.

Chapter

Gordie stared at the phone. "I'm not going to kiss Lucy Diaz, no matter how nice Ms. Tingle is."

Scratch put his head on the floor and thumped his tail.

Doug leaned back in his chair. "So you're going to kiss Lucy in front of the whole school. That's pretty brave of you, little brother."

Mom walked into the kitchen and poured herself a cup of coffee. "Who is kissing whom?"

"Gordie got the role of the prince in the

school play," said Doug. "He has to kiss Snow White, who is really Lucy Diaz."

"Great. Do you want me to start working on your costume?" asked Mom. "Maybe I should film the play."

Gordie grabbed Mom's hand. "Please don't, Mom."

"Why not?" Mom offered Gordie a Rice Krispies Treat. "You'll be able to watch it when you grow up."

Gordie slid into a kitchen chair. "I don't want to be in the play."

Mom sat down next to Gordie. "Ms. Tingle will be so disappointed. Do you want me to talk to her?"

Gordie sighed. Kids had to be careful when they talked to a mom. If you had a problem, moms wanted to fix it.

"How many lines do you have, Gordie?" asked Mom.

"I don't know." Gordie sighed. He took an apple from the bowl and then remembered that Snow White ate a poisoned apple. He put it back.

"Can you write Ms. Tingle a note and ask her if I can be an elf? Remind her that I ran off the stage last year."

Mom smiled. "But you'll make a very good prince. There are a lot of elves, but only one prince."

Gordie put his head down on the kitchen table. "I want to be an elf who doesn't kiss anyone."

Gordie jumped when the phone rang again.

Mom answered. "Hi, Lamont. Gordie's right here."

"Hi, Lamont."

"Hi. Do you want to shoot some hoops at the park?"

"No," said Gordie. "I just found out that I'm the prince in the play and Lucy is Snow White."

"You have to kiss Lucy?" Lamont screamed.

"Well, the prince has to kiss Snow White. But I'm only going to kiss her hand

or maybe I can just shake hands with her. I'll be a very polite prince."

"Good luck," said Lamont. "I'll see you tomorrow, Prince."

As soon as Gordie hung up, Mom walked over. "I'm sure Ms. Tingle only wants you to kiss Lucy's hand."

"Just make sure Lucy washes her hand first," added Doug.

"I'd rather wear tights than kiss Lucy Diaz," muttered Gordie.

Mom and Doug laughed. Scratch raised his head from the floor and thumped his tail. Gordie just went upstairs and stared out the window.

He wished he were back in the first grade. Being in the third grade was a lot of work.

Chapter 6

The next morning Gordie asked Mom to make him two garlic and sardine sand-wiches for his lunch. If he smelled really bad, Lucy might refuse to get near him.

Mom laughed and shook her head. "You'll get sick eating that, Gordie. I made you bologna and cheese."

Mom held up two brown bags. "You boys better hurry or you'll miss the bus."

Gordie wished he would miss the bus. He was afraid of hearing the next secret.

Doug stood up and took his bag. "Thanks, Mom. Bye, Scratch."

Scratch thumped his tail from under the kitchen table. Gordie bent down and patted his dog's head. Good old Scratch. He'd never run off and get married.

"Bring your script home, Gordie, and I'll help you with your lines," said Mom. "It will be fun. I'll be Snow White."

"I wish you could be."

Gordie had to run to catch the bus. He sat behind the driver and waited for Lamont's stop. He slid over when Lamont got on the bus. Lamont had white powder all over his face.

"Hey, Gordie," said Lamont. "Want part of my doughnut?"

Gordie shuddered. He never wanted to see another doughnut again.

Lamont popped the last of his doughnut into his mouth and brushed the powder from his pants. "Do I have any doughnut left on my face?"

"Your face has sugar on it."

"Ho, ho, ho," said Lamont. "Do I look like Santa?"

"I guess." Gordie leaned his head against the window. "Should we just ask Ms. Tingle if she's getting married?"

Lamont scratched his head. "A kid can't ask a teacher something like that."

"Lucy can ask her," said Gordie. "She always does stuff that a kid isn't supposed to do."

The bus pulled up in front of the school and stopped. Lamont and Gordie stopped talking and filed off the bus.

"There's Lucy," said Lamont. "Are you sure you don't want to ask for her help?"

"No . . . not unless we can't do it our-selves."

"What's our plan? Do we have one, Gordie?" Lamont looked worried.

"I'll have a plan by lunchtime, Lamont," said Gordie. "I promise."

The first bell rang, and the boys hur-ried inside. Gordie and Lamont had been best friends since kindergarten. Gordie had never broken a promise to him, and he didn't want to start now.

He had to come up with a plan to stop the wedding.

Chapter 7

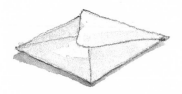

Gordie hurried into room nine. There was Ms. Tingle behind her desk, right where she belonged.

"Hi, Gordie. How are you this morning?"

"Fine." Gordie wasn't a bit fine.

"Good morning, Ms. Tingle." Lucy raced in and set her books on her desk. "I already know that I'm Snow White, and I told Gordie that he's my prince. My mom said I should call Gordie right away so he could start learning his lines because she's worried Gordie will mess up the whole play like he did last year in second grade."

Ms. Tingle held up her hand. "Lucy, slow down."

Lucy shook back her black hair and drew in a deep breath. "My mom and I saw you posting the cast list after school. I wasn't spying."

"I know. I hope everyone is happy with their parts in the play," said Ms. Tingle.

Lucy nodded. "I am. I'll be the best Snow White ever. I hope Gordie doesn't mess anything up. He was a crummy candy cane."

"Gordie will be fine," said Ms. Tingle.

"I won't run off the stage for your play, Ms. Tingle." Gordie walked to his desk. "I'm going to underline all of my lines right now."

Gordie sat down and began underlining his lines in the script. He didn't have that many lines, but he did have to kiss Lucy. That was bad enough.

"How many lines do you have?"

Gordie looked up. Lucy was leaning over him like a little teacher.

"Three," said Gordie.

Lucy crossed her arms. "You have five. I already counted. See, you're already messing up."

Gordie frowned. Lucy shouldn't be counting his lines. It felt like trespassing.

"Class, we are going to be very busy," said Ms. Tingle. "But I know we will all work together and get things ready for the play."

Lucy raised her hand and waved it around. She started talking before Ms.

Tingle even told her to. "Can I wear lipstick for the play? Snow White at Disney World had on lots of makeup."

Ms. Tingle smiled. "Sure. Everyone in the play will wear a little makeup, just like real actors do."

Gordie and Lamont looked at each other and tried not to laugh. Gordie might wear ChapStick, but he wouldn't wear lipstick.

Ms. Tingle got the cast list from the door and read everyone's name and role. Even though Gordie didn't want to be the prince, he was getting excited about the play.

"I already know all of my lines," called Lucy. "I learn things real fast."

"Then why don't you learn how to raise your hand, Lucy?" said Lamont. He slapped his hand over his mouth. "Sorry, Ms. Tingle. I forgot to raise my hand to say that."

Lucy grinned.

"Class, put your name on your script

and then, beside your name, put the name of the character you are playing," said Ms. Tingle.

Gordie printed his name and then, in capital letters, printed PRINCE. If Ms. Tingle loved this play so much, maybe she would want to do another play next year. Then she wouldn't move to Ohio.

Gordie heard a knock. He felt sick as Mr. Wilson walked in and handed

Ms. Tingle an envelope. They both laughed, and then Mr. Wilson walked out. Ms. Tingle put the envelope on her desk. She was still smiling when she told room nine to turn to page thirty-five in their science books.

Chapter 8

All through science and reading, Gordie stared at the envelope on Ms. Tingle's desk. What secret message was inside? Passing notes wasn't allowed in room nine. Ms. Tingle said she'd read the note to the whole class if she caught a note being passed. Gordie thought that was a pretty good rule. Would Ms. Tingle read her note aloud?

"Gordie!" Lamont yanked on the sleeve of Gordie's sweatshirt. "Come on, time to line up for lunch."

Gordie blinked and then followed Lamont up the aisle. He watched Ms. Tingle

put the envelope into her center desk drawer. "Let's go down and have a good lunch, class."

As they headed to the lunchroom, Lamont peeked inside his lunch bag. "Good. My mom packed me cream cheese and olives. Want to share?"

Gordie looked down at his empty hands. "I left my lunch in my desk."

Lucy wagged her finger at Gordie. "Just don't forget your lines for the play, Gordie. If you mess up, you'll mess me up."

"Oh, go eat an apple, Snow Flake," said Lamont. "Don't scare the worm while you're at it."

Lucy laughed. "I hope my brothers won't have to scare you, Lamont."

Lamont didn't look scared, but Gordie was. How mad would Lucy's brothers be if they heard that Gordie messed up the play and made her look dumb?

Gordie broke out of line and hurried over to Ms. Tingle. "Ms. Tingle, can I go back to the room and get my lunch from my desk?"

Ms. Tingle nodded. "Of course. Just make sure you close the door when you leave."

"Can I go with him?" asked Lamont.

"Gordie knows the way to his desk, Lamont," said Ms. Tingle.

"He better know his lines," muttered Lucy.

Gordie hurried back to room nine. As soon as he opened the door, he flipped on the lights. The room looked bigger without any kids in it. Gordie went to his desk and grabbed his lunch. As he walked up the aisle, he studied Ms. Tingle's desk. It looked nice and clean. Nothing was on the top except a small clock and a box of tissues.

Gordie looked at the open classroom door. The halls were quiet now. He walked around and looked at Ms. Tingle's chair.

Gordie glanced again at the open door. Then he quickly pulled out Ms. Tingle's chair and opened the center drawer.

"I just want to see the note," muttered Gordie. "I'm not going to read it or anything."

Gordie pulled out the envelope. He chewed his lip. The envelope wasn't even glued shut. Gordie stopped. He wasn't used to being sneaky. He put the note back into the center drawer and closed it. Then he picked up his lunch and left, remembering to close the door, just like Ms. Tingle had asked. As Gordie passed a trash can under the clock, he tossed his lunch bag inside. Even a jelly sandwich wouldn't have made it past the huge lump in his throat.

Chapter
9

"Hey, where's your lunch, Gordie?" Lamont scooted over as Gordie sat down beside him.

"I threw it out." Gordie sighed. "I'm not hungry."

Lamont laughed. "You should have given it to me. I'm always hungry. Did you at least peek inside and see what your mom packed?"

The word *peek* made Gordie feel guilty all over again. Should he tell Lamont what he almost did?

Maybe not. Lamont would think Gordie was a sneak.

"Where's your lunch?" asked Lucy. "I thought you packed today."

Gordie looked up and watched Lucy chew her peanut butter cracker.

She pushed a sandwich toward Gordie. "Here, have half of my sandwich. You can't get sick now or you won't be able to be my prince."

"Gordie's not sick, just worried, Lucy," said Lamont. "Hey, can I have some cookies?"

Lucy put her elbows on the table and leaned closer. "You can have all four of my cookies if you tell me why Gordie is worried."

"Mind your own business, Lucy," snapped Gordie. "Lamont doesn't want your cookies." He pushed them away.

"Yes, I do," said Lamont. He reached out and took the cookies.

"Tell me why Gordie is worried, and I'll throw in this red licorice," said Lucy. "And four corn curls."

Lamont ate one of the oatmeal cookies

in two big bites. "Good cookies, Lucy. Gordie wants to know what's in the envelope Mr. Wilson gave Ms. Tingle." Lamont brushed the crumbs from the table.

Gordie snapped, "I'm not worried about the envelope. It's probably just a menu from the cafeteria or something."

Lucy laughed. "You're nuts, Gordie. If it were a menu, Ms. Tingle would have put it up on the bulletin board like she always does."

Lamont nodded. "Lucy's right. If you put something in an envelope, it's more important."

"I bet Mr. Wilson is asking for a date. I bet he signed his name and put a heart around it," said Lucy. "A girl with red hair sent my brother a mushy note like that, and she put it into an envelope and taped it shut. Love letters are always sealed." Lucy giggled. "I bet Mr. Wilson sealed it with a big old kiss." Lucy kissed the back of her hand with a loud smack.

"Hey, Lucy," said Lamont. "Why don't

you kiss yourself in the play so Gordie won't have to?"

Lucy kissed her hand again. "Oh, please go on a date with me, Ms. Tingle. *Smack, smack, smack!*"

"You don't know anything, Lucy Diaz." Gordie pounded his fist on the table. "Ms. Tingle's note wasn't taped or stapled," said Gordie. "I could have pulled it right out."

Lucy stopped kissing her hand. "Oooooh, I'm telling. You went back into room nine and looked in her desk."

"Her desk?" asked Lamont. He shook his head. "Man, you are in real trouble. You could get kicked out of school for something like that."

"I didn't read it," whispered Gordie.

"Wait until I tell Ms. Tingle," said Lucy.

"Be quiet, Lucy," Lamont said. "If Gordie gets kicked out of room nine, who will be the prince? Do you want Mikey to kiss you awake?"

Lucy frowned. "Mikey always has a runny nose. I don't want that nose near me."

"I didn't read the note," whispered Gordie. "I don't even know the color of the paper."

"Ha!" said Lucy, waving her straw in the air. "But you know paper is inside. That has to mean something."

"You'd make a crummy cop, Lucy," said Lamont. "Come on, Gordie. Let's go outside and play kickball."

Lucy crossed her arms. "What will you guys give me if I go and peek at the note?"

"Nothing," said Lamont. "Who cares?"

Gordie looked down at his shoes. He cared.

"How will you peek?" asked Gordie.

Lucy stood up and shoved the rest of her lunch into the bag. "I'll think of a way. A way that won't get me kicked out of school."

Gordie didn't care if Lucy got kicked *out* of the third grade. He just wanted to keep Ms. Tingle *in* the third grade.

Chapter
10

Gordie had fun playing kickball with Lamont after lunch. But as soon as he walked
back into room nine, Gordie remembered
the envelope.

"Okay, take your seats and get out your
scripts," said Ms. Tingle. "Time to stop talking, class."

Gordie put his script on top of his desk.
Anyone could marry Mr. Wilson and move
to Ohio. Mr. Wilson could find someone
else; but Gordie could never find another
Ms. Tingle.

"Let's start on page five," said Ms. Tingle.
"Mikey, you, Lauren, Gordie, and Lucy

come up front. Lamont and Colin, stand by the fish tank."

Gordie walked up the aisle. Lucy raced up the aisle and grabbed Gordie's arm. He shook her off. Even the seven dwarfs would have kicked Lucy out of their home once she started bossing everyone around like she owned the whole forest.

"Gordie, I didn't get a chance to peek into the envelope," she whispered.

"Gordie, start reading your lines," said Ms. Tingle. "Lucy, pretend you have already eaten the poisoned apple. Lie down on the craft table and wait for Gordie, I mean your prince, to come over."

Lucy nodded. "Okay, Ms. Tingle. Should I look like I'm in pain? Did the poisoned apple make me throw up or just make me go into a coma?"

Ms. Tingle smiled. "You are not in pain, Lucy. Just lie down on the table and pretend you're sleeping."

Gordie looked down at his script. He had to walk over to Lucy and say, "Oh, who

is this lovely maiden? Perhaps a kiss will awaken her?"

Gordie knew his lines were really mushy. His brother and the rest of the fifth-graders would laugh. Lumpy Labriola would probably boo and stomp his feet.

"Gordie?" Ms. Tingle said. "It's your line."

Gordie nodded. "Sorry."

Lucy sat up on the craft table. "I've been asleep for two minutes already. See, Ms.

Tingle, Gordie forgot his lines. And he has his script right in his hand. He is going to really mess up this whole play, and my aunt is flying in from New Hampshire just to watch me be Snow White—"

Ms. Tingle held up her hand. "Lucy, lie back down and pretend you are asleep. You are so deep in sleep that you can't say a single word."

Lamont clapped. "Let's give Lucy an apple every day."

Ms. Tingle frowned. "Lamont, don't make me flash the lights to get your attention. I want to finish this rehearsal, okay?"

Lamont nodded. "Sorry, Ms. Tingle."

Ms. Tingle looked down at her clipboard. "Okay, Gordie. Walk over and pretend that you're just looking for some water for your horse. Then you see Snow White, and you're concerned."

"And maybe the prince thinks the seven dwarfs gave her a sleeping pill so she would finally stop talking for a while," said Mikey.

Lots of kids laughed. Gordie saw Ms. Tingle smile, but then she must have remembered she was a teacher and tried to look mad.

"Class, we only have two weeks to get this play ready." Ms. Tingle looked tired. "I want to count the number of days left to rehearse. Gordie, can you get my calendar from my middle drawer?"

Gordie opened the center drawer of Ms. Tingle's desk. He picked up the calendar and then saw the envelope Mr. Wilson had given her.

"Gordie, would you also bring over my red pen?" Ms. Tingle asked.

"Okay," said Gordie. He picked up a pen. Then he glanced down at the envelope. Part of the note was sticking out. Gordie slowly closed the drawer, but looked down at the papers. In large black letters he read: GUEST LIST: TINGLE/WILSON WEDDING. DECEMBER 17.

December 17? That was only a few weeks away. Gordie slammed the desk

drawer so fast that Ms. Tingle looked up
from her script.

"Sorry," muttered Gordie. Ms. Tingle
must have thought he was apologizing for
slamming her drawer. Maybe teachers had
to pay for broken desks. But Gordie wasn't
a bit sorry about slamming her drawer. He
was only sorry that Ms. Tingle was plan-
ning a wedding that room nine wasn't
even invited to.

"Gordie, get over here," said Lucy. "The craft table isn't the most comfortable bed, you know."

"Take another bite of your apple, Snow Flake," said Lamont.

Gordie walked over and handed Ms. Tingle the pen and calendar. "Here's your pen. It was right under the envelope in your desk."

"Thanks, Gordie." Ms. Tingle clicked on the pen and opened her calendar book.

"The big envelope, Ms. Tingle," Gordie said.

"Ms. Tingle," said Lucy. "I don't think a real prince would keep Snow White waiting like this."

"Say your line, Gordie," said Ms. Tingle as she scribbled something on her calendar.

"Okay, okay," muttered Gordie. He glanced down at his script as he walked over to the craft table. Lucy lay back down and folded her hands on her chest.

"Lucy, go back and say your line again;

then take a bite of the apple," said Ms. Tingle. "Set the apple down, yawn, and lie down."

Lucy nodded. "Should I let the apple roll across the room? Or should I keep the apple in my hand to remind the audience that it's poisoned?"

"Why don't you put the apple into your mouth and keep it there, Lucy?" suggested Lamont.

"Why don't you all behave," said Ms. Tingle. "We have only two weeks to get this play into good shape."

Gordie held up his script and read. "Oh, my, who is this lovely maiden?"

Lucy sat up. "Wait until I say my line first, Gordie." Lucy took a bite of her apple. "It was so nice of the old lady to give me this apple. It is so sweet and . . ."

Lucy stretched and yawned. "I am so sleepy." Lucy stretched out on the table and began to snore.

Gordie looked over at Ms. Tingle. "Does Snow White snore?"

"I'm snoring so the audience doesn't think I'm dead," snapped Lucy. "Don't tell me how to be a good Snow White, Gordie."

"Go on with your line, Gordie," said Ms. Tingle. She rubbed her head like room nine was giving her a giant headache.

"Oh, my, who is this lovely maiden?" said Gordie.

Lucy snored more loudly.

Gordie chewed his lip. "Perhaps a kiss will awaken her."

Lucy opened one eye.

"Does Gordie really have to kiss her?" asked Lamont.

Ms. Tingle sighed. "Just kiss her hand, Gordie."

A few kids started to laugh.

"I want everyone in room nine to take this play seriously," said Ms. Tingle. "It will only work if we all work together."

Gordie was just about to kiss Lucy's hand, to make Ms. Tingle feel better, when the classroom door opened. Mr. Wilson walked in without knocking.

Chapter
11

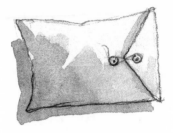

Lucy poked Gordie's side. "Are you going to kiss my hand so I can wake up and get off this craft table?"

Gordie watched as Ms. Tingle talked quietly to Mr. Wilson, then walked over to her desk and handed him the envelope.

Good, thought Gordie. Give him back the wedding list and tell him to stay out of room nine.

Mr. Wilson held up the envelope and smiled. "See you on Friday."

"Seven thirty," said Ms. Tingle. "I'm really looking forward to it, Leo."

Leo? That wasn't a bit teacherlike.

"Gordie!" Lucy held out her hand. "Come on."

Gordie ignored Lucy. He wasn't going to kiss her hand unless Ms. Tingle saw it. He didn't want to waste a kiss.

After Mr. Wilson left, Ms. Tingle kept smiling. All she cared about was meeting Mr. Wilson on Friday at seven thirty.

"Ms. Tingle, Gordie won't kiss my hand," whined Lucy. "I don't think he's a very good prince, do you?"

Ms. Tingle kept smiling. "Gordie's a fine prince." She glanced at her watch. "We better get ready for art class."

"Should Gordie kiss my hand first?" asked Lucy.

"Put your scripts away," said Ms. Tingle.

Lucy hopped off the table and kissed her own hand. "You're a crummy prince, Gordie. You better not mess up the play or else."

Or else what? wondered Gordie. Lucy

was always saying "or else," like she was in charge of everyone.

Gordie slumped into his chair and stared at the back of Lucy's head. He could hardly wait until school was over so he could tell Lamont about the wedding list. He wouldn't tell Lucy and that would drive her nuts. Lucy wasn't the only one in room nine with a big secret.

Gordie was feeling a lot better about things until Lucy turned around and knocked on his desk.

"Guess what I know that you don't," she whispered. "It's my best secret ever."

"I have a secret, too," said Gordie. "It's much better than yours."

Lucy smiled like she didn't believe a word. She smiled real mean, like she knew Gordie's secret was really dumb.

"Tell me your little secret, and I'll tell you my important one," offered Lucy.

"Maybe," said Gordie.

Lucy sighed. "My secret is so private

that my very own mother told me not to tell anyone."

"So why are you going to tell me, Lucy?"

Lucy frowned. "I don't know. I guess I want to tell you so I won't be so worried. It's about Ms. Tingle."

Gordie leaned closer. Had Lucy seen the wedding list, too?

"Okay, I'll tell you," said Lucy. "I'll even tell Lamont because you two are good at being sneaky. I think we'll need a real sneaky plan."

"A plan for what?" Gordie never thought he'd be part of a plan with Lucy. It was bad enough he had to kiss her hand.

Lucy glanced over at Ms. Tingle. "My mom and I saw Ms. Tingle at the mall yesterday."

"So what?" Even teachers were allowed to shop.

Lucy sighed. "She was looking at wedding dresses."

Gordie stared down at his desk. Lucy's

secret and Gordie's were almost the same. It was time for Gordie and Lucy to work together to dream up a way to keep Ms. Tingle in room nine and away from Ohio. It was going to take a very, very sneaky plan.

Chapter 12

Gordie was the first one out of his seat when the dismissal bell finally rang. Lucy was right behind him as they went out into the hall to go to their locker.

"We better tell Lamont," whispered Lucy. She opened the locker and got out her pink sweatshirt. "We're going to need all the help we can get."

"We can tell him outside, before we get on the bus," Gordie whispered back.

"I'll meet you both by the fire hydrant," said Lucy before she grabbed her back-pack and hurried down the crowded hall.

"Hey, Gordie," said Lamont. "I saw you

in a huddle with Snow Flake. What's going on?"

Gordie grabbed his jacket and closed the locker. "Meet me outside by the fire hydrant."

"What's with all this secret stuff?" asked Lamont.

Gordie looked around, and then lowered his voice. "Room nine is in serious trouble."

Lamont nodded. "Rehearsal was bad today, but don't worry about the play. I'm sure it will be okay in two weeks."

"Meet me at the hydrant. Lucy is waiting for us." Gordie grabbed his backpack and walked quickly outside.

Gordie and Lucy didn't say a word until Lamont joined them a few minutes later.

"What is going on?" asked Lamont. "We're going to miss our bus, Gordie. Are you two mad at each other about the play?"

Gordie shook his head. "It's not about the play, Lamont. Lucy saw Ms. Tingle looking at wedding dresses."

"And she tried on a veil, too. She and this other lady were twirling around like they were playing dress-up," added Lucy.

Lamont hitched his backpack higher on his shoulders. "So what? My sister and her friends always look at wedding dresses. No big deal."

"It's a big deal when you're a grown-up," said Lucy. "They had a salesgirl with them and everything."

Gordie glanced over at the kids boarding the school bus. "Lucy's right, Lamont. This is a big deal."

"I wanted to go over and ask Ms. Tingle what she was doing, but my mom told me it was none of my business," said Lucy. "Ms. Tingle *is* our business."

Lamont laughed. "If Ms. Tingle were getting married, she'd tell us. You can't keep something like that a secret."

"Ms. Tingle *is* getting married," said Gordie. "I saw the wedding list in her desk drawer."

Lucy tossed back her hair. "That does

it. We have to organize our plan. I don't want Ms. Tingle to get married until I'm out of the third grade."

"How can we stop her?" asked Lamont.

"Maybe we could tell the principal. He could stop her," suggested Gordie. "Remember when he made the second grade teacher take down the cornstalks from her door because they were a fire hazard?

"Maybe we could make up a rule, and Ms. Tingle and Mr. Wilson can read it and then worry that they will get in trouble. They could think Mr. Frattaroli will fire them for wasting school time by being in love with each other."

"Yeah, or we could pour syrup over all the computers, and Mr. Wilson will be fired for being a bad computer teacher," added Lucy.

"Or we could write Ms. Tingle a mean note," said Lamont. "We could say, 'Dear Ms. Tingle, Roses are red, violets are pink, you think you're cute, but I think you stink.'" Lamont grinned. "Then we'll sign

Mr. Wilson's name. We could type it on the computer and put it on her desk."

Lucy smiled. "I like that plan. We could write her a new note every day until Ms. Tingle gets so mad she rips up the wedding list."

"I don't know," said Gordie. "The notes would really hurt Ms. Tingle's feelings. She's so nice to everyone."

"Exactly," said Lucy. "Which is why we want her for ourselves."

"What if she cries?" asked Gordie. "I bet no one has ever told Ms. Tingle that she stinks."

"Well, we need a plan right away," said Lucy. "We better get on our buses before we miss them."

Gordie knew Lucy was right. They needed a plan right away, even if it was a sneaky, mean plan. As he ran for his bus, he decided to do whatever it took to keep Ms. Tingle in room nine, where she belonged.

Chapter

13

Gordie slid onto the bus seat and made room for Lamont. "Lamont, do you want to come to my house so we can work on the plan?"

Before Lamont could answer, Lumpy Labriola got on the bus and walked right over to Gordie and Lamont.

"Ho, ho," said Lumpy. "Things are getting pretty serious, lover boy. I saw you talking to the little woman. Next thing you know, you and Lucy will be picking out your wedding invitations."

"We were just talking about the play, Lumpy," said Lamont.

"Oh, listen to the best man sticking up for the nervous groom." Lumpy walked to the back of the bus, singing, "Here comes the bride, right by Gordie's side."

Gordie stared out the bus window. "Boy, this has been a real lousy day. All anyone can think about are weddings."

Lamont nodded. "I'm not getting married for at least fifty years."

"I'm never getting married," said Gordie. "Not even if I got to eat a twenty-layer cake."

"You can have some of my wedding cake," promised Lamont.

Gordie smiled. "Thanks. What kind of cake do you think Ms. Tingle will have?"

"A computer cake. Maybe with a little mouse on the top."

Gordie turned around and saw Lumpy singing in the back of the bus. Now the whole bus thought Gordie was going to marry Lucy.

"Are you going to call Lucy when you get home?" asked Lamont.

Gordie shrugged. "I don't know. I guess so. She doesn't want Ms. Tingle to get married. No one does."

Lamont laughed. "Mr. Wilson does!"

"It's not funny, Lamont. Let's hope that Lucy can help us come up with a good plan."

When Gordie got off the bus ten minutes later, he was feeling better. The sun was out, and he wanted to take Scratch to the park to play. He raced up the driveway and heard the phone ringing.

As soon as he walked into the kitchen, Mom handed him the phone.

"Hello?"

"I have the perfect plan." It was Lucy.

"What is it?" Gordie had to admit that Lucy was a fast worker.

"I am going to type up a list of teacher rules. It'll have rules like, 'Don't run in the halls,' and 'Don't chew gum in the classroom.' Stuff like that."

"Ms. Tingle doesn't do any of that

stuff." Maybe Lucy's plan was a silly one after all. No wonder she thought of it so quickly.

"Wait," said Lucy. "I didn't get to the good part yet. So after three or four rules, I'm going to add, 'Teachers are not allowed to date each other.'"

"How will Ms. Tingle see the rules?" asked Gordie.

"That's where you and Lamont can help. As soon as we get to school tomorrow, I'll give you the list, and you two can sneak into the teachers' lounge and hang it on their bulletin board."

"Are you crazy?" sputtered Gordie.

"Gordie," said Mom. "Are you okay?"

Gordie nodded. He wasn't a bit okay, but he didn't want to tell his mom what was going on in room nine. Besides, Gordie didn't even know what was going on.

"I'll see you tomorrow," said Lucy before she hung up.

Gordie kept the phone to his ear until

the operator told him to please hang up if he wanted to make a call.

Gordie couldn't eat his after-school snack. At dinner he couldn't finish his hamburger. In the morning Gordie could barely swallow his Cheerios.

Lucy was nuts if she thought he was going to sneak into the teachers' lounge and tack up a fake list of rules. What if he got caught? He'd get kicked out of the third grade. Ms. Tingle would be sad. She always said she wanted to be proud of the kids in room nine.

"Hey, what's wrong with you?" asked Doug. "Sorry I teased you about Lucy. I was only kidding. I know she drives you crazy."

Gordie sipped his juice and nodded. "Sometimes she's okay."

Gordie stood up and grabbed his lunch. "Bye, Mom. You're the best. Thanks for everything you do for me."

Mom reached out and hugged Gordie.

"You're welcome for everything, honey. You sound like you're not going to see me for a week or two!"

Gordie hugged his mom back. If he got caught in the teachers' lounge, she could be right.

Chapter
14

Gordie slid over in his seat as soon as Lamont got on the bus. He hadn't been able to call Lamont and tell him about Lucy's plan. Every time he picked up the phone, Mom, Dad, or Doug would walk in.

"Hey, Gordie," said Lamont. He held out a jelly doughnut. "Want a bite?"

"Doughnuts make me sick." Gordie waited until Lamont swallowed his last bite before he told him the plan.

"Lucy wants us to do *what*?" shouted Lamont.

"Shhh," warned Gordie. He glanced behind him to make sure Lumpy wasn't listening. "I don't want to do it, either. But it's the only plan we have. We're running out of time, Lamont."

"Man." Lamont leaned back in his seat and groaned. "My mom will kill me if I get caught and sent to some school jail."

"There's a school jail?" Gordie had never heard of one, but it sounded like there must be.

Lamont and Gordie didn't talk for the rest of the bus ride. As soon as they got off the bus, Lucy would be waiting for them with the list of fake rules.

The bus pulled up in front of the school. Even though Lamont and Gordie sat right behind the bus driver, they were the last to get off.

The boys watched as the bus pulled slowly away. Gordie wished he could have stayed on it.

"There you are!"

Gordie turned around. Lucy held out the list.

"Hurry up. When the first bell rings, all the teachers will be in their classrooms. Then you two can hang the rules on the bulletin board in the teachers' lounge."

Lamont looked over his shoulder. "Shhh. We can't do this, Lucy."

"It's dangerous," added Gordie.

Lucy stomped her foot. "You big babies. You mean I did all this work for nothing?"

Gordie looked down at his shoes. He didn't want Ms. Tingle to walk down the aisle, and he didn't want to get Lucy mad, but he really didn't want to end up in some school jail.

"I've done my job," snapped Lucy. She handed Gordie the list of rules. "The rest is up to you."

Gordie watched as Lucy stormed across the playground, her black hair bouncing up and down with each step.

Lamont looked down at the list in Gordie's hand. "What are you going to do now?"

Gordie shrugged. What he wanted to do was to get back on the bus and go home. But it was too late for that now.

The first bell rang and Gordie headed to the front steps. He folded the list of rules and put it in his pocket. It was only a thin sheet of paper, but it felt like it weighed a hundred pounds. Lucy said the rest of the plan was up to him. Would he be able to make it work?

Chapter

15

Gordie took his time walking to his locker. He took five sips of water from the fountain in the hall, and then he retied his sneakers two times.

"We're going to be late, Gordie," said Lamont as he closed his locker.

"I'm thinking," whispered Gordie. He was thinking that he wanted to throw Lucy's dumb rules into the trash can.

"Well, count me out of whatever you think up," said Lamont.

When the second bell rang, Gordie hurried into room nine. Lucy smiled as he walked by her, and then frowned after he shook his head.

"Chicken," she whispered.

Gordie slid into his seat. He'd rather be a chicken than a sneak.

"Class, let's get settled," said Ms. Tingle. "We want to finish our studies so we can spend more time on our play. We can go onstage today."

A few kids clapped. Lucy waved her hand.

"Can we wear our costumes? My mom can bring mine over. She won't mind at all."

"We'll wear costumes at dress rehearsal, Lucy," said Ms. Tingle.

Twenty minutes later, Ms. Tingle was busy printing spelling words on the board. Gordie leaned forward and looked at her hands. She didn't have a ring on her left or right hand. That was a good sign. Or maybe it was a bad sign. Mr. Wilson could be waiting for the wedding to give her a ring. Maybe Mr. Wilson didn't like to spend money. He gave Ms. Tingle only one dough-nut, not a dozen. Ms. Tingle was so nice she deserved lots of doughnuts and lots of diamond rings.

When it was time to line up for gym, Gordie raised his hand.

"Can I go to the restroom?"

"Yes, but hurry," said Ms. Tingle. She smiled. "You don't want to be late for gym."

Gordie walked as fast as he could. Once the bathroom door closed, Gordie checked under each stall. He was alone. He pulled out the list.

NEW RULES FOR TEACHERS

1. *DO NOT USE TOO MUCH PAPER. IT COSTS MONEY.*

2. *DO NOT PUT SODA CANS IN WITH PAPER TRASH.*

3. *DO NOT RUN IN THE HALLS.*

4. *DO NOT YELL AT YOUR STUDENTS UNLESS THEY ARE REALLY IN TROUBLE.*

5. *DO NOT PASS NOTES WHILE YOU ARE SUPPOSED TO BE TEACHING.*

6. *DO NOT DATE OR MARRY ANY OTHER TEACHER!!*

Gordie read the list six or seven times before he crumpled it up into a tight ball. He put it into the trash can by the sinks.

"That won't work," muttered Gordie. "The janitor might find it and hang it up in the teachers' lounge."

Gordie got the list from the trash can and looked around the bathroom.

Two loud knocks on the door made Gordie jump.

"Time for gym," Ms. Tingle called.

"I'll be right out, Ms. Tingle," Gordie called back.

"Is everything okay?" she asked.

"Sure."

Gordie unrolled the tight ball. A little first- or second-grader walked in, staring at Gordie.

"Hi," said Gordie as he raced into the first stall.

Gordie crumpled the teacher list again and tossed it into the toilet. Then he closed his eyes and flushed. He only opened his eyes when he felt water splashing over his shoes. That's when he saw the toilet over-flowing and the teacher rules spinning around and around on top.

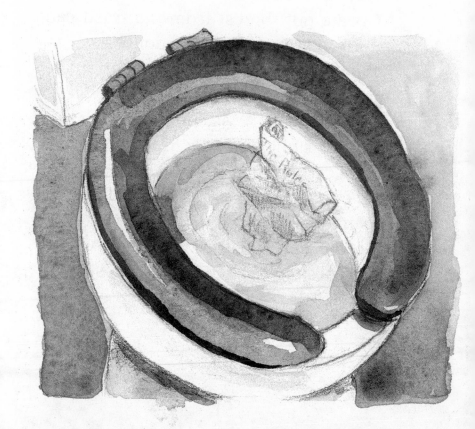

Chapter
16

The little kid raced out of his stall and started yelling. "It's a flood! I didn't do it!"

Gordie shook off his sneakers. "It's okay."

Before Gordie could even get out of the stall, Lamont raced into the bathroom.

"What's all the yelling about, Gordie? Ms. Tingle told me to come in and get you. . . . Where did all the water come from?"

The little kid tugged on Lamont's shirt. "I didn't do it." He looked at Gordie and ran out of the bathroom.

"We better get the janitor," said Gordie. "The toilet went nuts on me."

"I'll get him," said Lamont.

As soon as Lamont left, Gordie picked up the teacher list. He turned his face away and shook it. Then he went to the trash can. He wanted to get rid of it before Mr. Matlock, the janitor, came in to inspect the mess. What if Mr. Matlock decided to empty the can while he was here and found the list? Gordie heard voices in the hall and quickly shoved the soggy list under the metal trash can.

The heavy wooden door opened. "What's the problem?" asked Mr. Matlock. He was carrying a bucket and had a mop slung across his shoulder. He eyed the water and then Gordie. "You didn't try to flush down a bad spelling paper, did you?"

Gordie shook his head.

Mr. Matlock set the bucket down and went inside the stall. After a few minutes he came out, drying his hands on a rag. "It's fixed. Go back to class."

"Sorry," said Gordie. He glanced at the trash can. If Mr. Matlock left now, he could get the list and put it in his locker.

"Don't use so much paper next time," said Mr. Matlock. "It always gets you in trouble."

Lamont eyed Gordie as they walked out into the hall. "What did you do?"

Gordie sighed. "I tried to flush the fake

list down the toilet. Now it's under the trash can. I have to get it and take it home."

"Everything okay, boys?" asked Ms. Tingle from the head of the line.

"Just a little water," said Lamont.

Lucy reached out and grabbed Gordie's arm as he passed her. "Is the list okay? Did you put it where it's supposed to be?"

Gordie shook his head even though he thought the list was *exactly* where it was supposed to be: not in the teachers' lounge, but *almost* in the trash.

Chapter 17

As soon as they got into the gym, Lucy raced over to Gordie. "What did you do with the list?"

"It fell into the toilet."

Lucy skidded to a stop. "The toilet? It's supposed to be in the teachers' lounge. That was the plan."

"We need another plan," whispered Gordie.

Lucy frowned. "We're running out of time. You messed up again."

"I did not." Gordie barely whispered this since he knew Lucy was right.

All through gym class Lucy kept shoot-

ing the basketball at Gordie. He kept ducking, knowing she was mad.

"Okay, listen up," said Mrs. Johnson. She blasted her whistle. "I want you to run down the gym, dribbling the ball. At the black line, pass the ball to the person to your left. Not your right, but your left."

Another blast of the whistle sent three lines of kids down the gym floor. Gordie was first, dribbling against Lucy to his right. She glared at him.

When Gordie reached the black line, he stopped and bounced the ball to his left. Instead of Mikey catching the ball, Mr. Matlock did. He caught the ball with one hand. Mr. Matlock didn't look too happy. Gordie didn't look too happy, either.

Mrs. Johnson lifted her whistle and put it to her mouth when Ms. Tingle walked into the gym. Gordie glanced over at Lucy and Lamont.

Ms. Tingle walked toward Gordie.

"Gordie, come with me."

Gordie followed Ms. Tingle out into the hall. Would Mr. Matlock tell Ms. Tingle that Gordie was plotting to mess up her wedding plans?

Chapter
18

Gordie's legs felt rubbery as he, Mr. Matlock, and Ms. Tingle reached the hall.

"Gordie, we need to ask you something," said Ms. Tingle.

"We brought you out here because we don't want the other kids to hear," said Mr. Matlock. "I found something in the bathroom."

"Okay," said Gordie. Should he confess first?

Mr. Matlock reached into his back pocket. "Is this yours?"

Gordie closed his eyes, and then opened them. Should he tell them that Lucy was the one who wrote the list? Should he take the blame for everyone?

"Is this yours?" Mr. Matlock asked again.

Gordie looked up at Mr. Matlock. "What?"

"I found this twenty-dollar bill in the restroom. It was behind the clogged toilet. Is it yours?"

Gordie grinned. He was never so happy to say, "No."

Ms. Tingle smiled back. "We wanted to ask you first before we left the money in the office."

Gordie went back into gym class, feeling as light as a feather. The fake list had not been found. He would get the list, bring it home, and bury it in the backyard.

Gordie managed to ignore Lucy for the rest of the day. He ignored the dirty looks she kept sending his way. Rehearsal went really well. It was fun to be on a real stage, under the lights.

At the end of the day, Ms. Tingle was

smiling a lot. "Study your lines well tonight, class. Tomorrow we'll start rehearsals without the script."

"I'm ready," said Lucy. "You can give me more lines if you want, Ms. Tingle."

"Just polish the lines you already have, Lucy." Ms. Tingle turned off the stage lights. "Let's get back to class. We still have schoolwork to finish."

"When are we going to bring in our costumes?" asked Leslie. "My mom finished my queen outfit last night."

"Bring all costumes in on Friday," said Ms. Tingle. "We can have a dress rehearsal then so each of you will be relaxed the day of the play."

"I'm already relaxed," announced Lucy.

"Then stop talking so I can relax," said Lamont. "I can hardly wait until you take a bite of that apple and conk out."

Gordie laughed, and then remembered he had to give the kiss that would wake Lucy up.

Just then, Mr. Wilson walked into room nine.

"Finish page sixteen, class," said Ms. Tingle. She turned and smiled at Mr. Wilson.

Gordie looked down at his desk. Maybe Ms. Tingle really did like Mr. Wilson.

"Oh, no!" cried Ms. Tingle.

Gordie looked up. Mr. Wilson was patting Ms. Tingle's hand. Her face was bright red.

Lucy turned around and raised her eyebrows at Gordie. Lamont leaned over and poked him on the arm.

"Did you get rid of the list?" whispered Lamont.

Gordie scratched his head, watching Ms. Tingle's face getting redder and redder. Now Mr. Wilson turned his back to the class and talked in low tones to Ms. Tingle.

Had the janitor found the note, dried it off, and hung it in the teachers' lounge?

Was Ms. Tingle upset because she thought she couldn't marry Mr. Wilson?

Gordie raised his hand. He had to go to the restroom and make sure the note was still under the trash can. And if it was, he'd rip it into a million pieces so no one would be able to put it back together again.

Ms. Tingle was too sad to notice his hand. Gordie got out of his seat and hurried to her desk. He was just about to ask if he could use the bathroom pass, when Mr. Wilson reached into his pocket and handed Ms. Tingle an envelope.

"This should explain it all. We have to work quickly," he said quietly before he turned and left the room.

Ms. Tingle stared at the envelope and then put it into her black purse.

"Can I go to the restroom?" Gordie asked. He had to work quickly, too.

Ms. Tingle handed him the wooden bathroom pass. She didn't smile like she usually did or tell him to hurry back.

Gordie walked to the restroom as quickly as he could. He pushed open the heavy wooden door. The trash can was still there. The floor was dry. Gordie looked under the stalls. Good, no feet. He walked back to the trash can and lifted it up.

The list was gone!

Chapter
19

A few days later, Ms. Tingle talked to the class about the play.

"The play gets closer every day," she said. "I am so proud of all of you for learning your lines and bringing in such great costumes."

"My mom hired a lady to finish mine," announced Lucy. "The material was very expensive and not even on sale."

"It's lovely, Lucy." Ms. Tingle picked up her script.

"You wrote a good play, Ms. Tingle," said Gordie. "Even the fifth-graders will clap."

Gordie was glad to see Ms. Tingle smiling again. Maybe she finally got used to the idea that she wasn't allowed to marry Mr. Wilson.

When room nine walked down the hall to the library, Gordie noticed the door to the teachers' lounge was open. It was usually closed.

"Hey, the door's open," whispered Lamont. "Look, they have a soda machine and a microwave. Maybe I'll be a teacher when I grow up. I'd pop corn all day."

Gordie slowed down. He craned his head and tried to see what was on the bulletin board. He wished he had binoculars. Just as he was reading the notices, Ms. Schano, the librarian, walked out into the hall.

"Hello, Ms. Schano. Can I turn my class over to you now?" asked Ms. Tingle. "We were on our way to the library."

"Of course." Ms. Schano smiled. "I just shelved twenty new books. Let's go see the new additions to our library."

"Gordie, did you see the teacher rules on the bulletin board in the teachers' lounge?" Lamont whispered.

"I'm not sure—" began Gordie.

Lucy spun around. "So you did hang it up, Gordie! Why didn't you tell me?"

"Because it's none of your business, Snow Flake," said Lamont.

"It *is* my business because I wrote the teacher rules," said Lucy. "If the plan works, it's all because of me."

Lamont yawned. "Remind me to clap."

Gordie watched Ms. Tingle walk down the hall. She looked sad again. He wanted to tell her that the list of rules was a fake and if she really wanted to marry Mr. Wilson, then Gordie would be happy for her.

Gordie walked into the library and listened as Ms. Schano talked about the new books. She was so excited about the books that Gordie got excited, too. He was trying to decide which book to check out when he felt a heavy hand on his shoulder. Gordie looked up into Mr. Wilson's smiling face.

"Excuse me, Ms. Schano. Can I talk to Gordie for a minute?" asked Mr. Wilson.

"No," said Gordie. "I mean, yes." Gordie got up and followed Mr. Wilson to the corner of the library.

"I want you to help me with a little surprise," said Mr. Wilson. "I don't want to take up your library time, but come up to the computer room after lunch. It will only take a few minutes."

Gordie nodded. A few minutes was all it would take for Mr. Wilson to kick Gordie out of the third grade for messing up his wedding with Ms. Tingle.

Chapter

20

Gordie was checking out two library books when Lucy walked over.

"What did Mr. Wilson say to you?" she asked. "Did he find out that you snuck into the teachers' lounge? I used my own computer so I don't want them to trace it back to me. But your fingerprints are all over it. I could always say you came into my house and used my computer."

Gordie shoved past Lucy. "This whole plan was your idea, Lucy. If I get in trouble, then you should get in trouble. Your plan was stupid."

Lucy followed Gordie. "The plan worked, so it was a good plan."

"Leave me alone, Lucy." Gordie gathered up his books. "If I'm not back in the classroom after lunch, it's because Mr. Wilson kicked me out of the third grade for messing up his life."

"I don't think he can do that without asking your parents first," said Lucy. "He's only a computer teacher, not a principal."

"Maybe my parents *are* in the computer room right now, asking Mr. Wilson not to send me to jail," said Gordie. "Or, maybe my dad is in room nine, cleaning out my desk, wondering if he has enough money to send me to military school."

Lucy laughed. "You're crazy, Gordie."

Gordie gripped his books. "Mind your own business, okay Lucy? Just mind your own Snow Flake business."

Lucy turned and stomped off. Gordie walked back to his table and put his head down. He didn't want to go visit Mr. Wilson. He was worn out. Maybe he should go to

Mr. Wilson right now and confess about the fake teacher rules.

After lunch, Gordie went upstairs. Mr. Wilson was standing outside the computer room, rubbing his hands together. He smiled and smoothed back his black hair. "Gordie, let's talk about Ms. Tingle."

Gordie dashed to the water fountain and gulped down a gallon of water. Maybe he should ask for his parents, or a lawyer.

Gordie followed Mr. Wilson into the computer room, glad that he didn't see his

parents, the principal, or any cops. He was especially glad that he didn't see Ms. Tingle, looking disappointed in him for being a sneaky kid.

Mr. Wilson sat on the edge of his desk, just the way Ms. Tingle did.

"Gordie, you know how excited Ms. Tingle is about the big event, don't you?"

Gordie swallowed. The big event? The wedding, which would turn Ms. Tingle into Mrs. Wilson?

"She is real happy about it," said Gordie. "Or, she used to be real happy about it." Gordie ripped the skin around his thumb. Mr. Wilson knew about the fake list. He knew Gordie was the one to blame for its being tacked up in the teachers' lounge.

"Can you help me surprise her?" asked Mr. Wilson. He got off the desk and opened his center desk drawer. He pulled out a large square envelope. Gordie swallowed. Was Mr. Wilson going to make him sign a confession?

Gordie stared at the envelope. Maybe he should ask for one phone call.

"I bought this card for Ms. Tingle to congratulate her for writing such a great play. Could you get everyone in room nine to sign it? You can give it to her onstage, right after the play."

Gordie slumped with relief. "Sure. I can do that."

"Great." Mr. Wilson handed Gordie the envelope. "I didn't want to give you this in front of Ms. Tingle. Let's keep it a secret."

Gordie nodded. Secrets were his specialty.

"Thank you, Gordie," said Mr. Wilson. "Ms. Tingle has said so many nice things about you that I knew I could trust you."

Gordie's cheeks flushed warm as he headed out into the hall, knowing he shouldn't be trusted at all. He was probably the sneakiest kid in room nine.

Chapter
21

Gordie got a pencil from his locker. He went outside to the playground so he could get lots of kids to sign Ms. Tingle's card. Gordie didn't want to take a chance of forgetting anyone's signature. Maybe Ms. Tingle would love the card so much she would take it with her when she moved to Ohio.

"There's Gordie!" cried Lucy. She tossed back her hair and charged across the playground with Lamont, Mikey, and Leslie following.

"What happened with Mr. Wilson?" asked Lamont. "Are you in trouble?"

"No. Mr. Wilson wants everyone in room nine to sign a card for Ms. Tingle." Gordie held up the card and pencil.

"You're not in trouble, right?" asked Lucy.

"No." Not yet, thought Gordie.

Lucy stepped so close to Gordie he could smell her gum.

"If you get kicked out of school, I'll need a new prince for the play."

"Mr. Wilson just wants us to sign the card."

Lucy snatched the card. "Let me sign first."

Gordie handed her the pencil.

"A pencil?" Lucy frowned. "You can't sign a fancy card with a chewed-up pencil, Gordie. You need a sparkly pen, or a Magic Marker. This pencil is junk."

"Just sign it, Lucy," said Lamont. "The bell's about to ring."

"Okay," sighed Lucy. "Turn around, Gordie, so I can use your back."

Lamont used Gordie's back next. Pretty

soon Lucy had rounded up another ten people to sign the card. Gordie's back was getting worn out.

"Can't we use Lamont's back now?" asked Gordie.

"Just a few more kids, Gordie," said Lucy. "Hey, Laura and Paul, come on over."

By the time the recess bell rang, the card had sixteen signatures. Gordie stood up and rubbed his back.

"Well, it's too bad we had to use your pencil, instead of a glitter pen," said Lucy. "But the card still looks good."

Lamont laughed. "Aren't you going to sign it, Gordie?"

Lucy handed him the card. "Flip it over since the front is pretty crowded."

Gordie studied the card. Lucy's name was in big letters, right in the center. She had drawn a crown on top of the letter *L*. Lucy was such a look-at-me kind of girl.

"Sign next to me, buddy," said Lamont. He pointed to his name. Lamont had drawn a Santa cap on top of the *O* in his name. Lots of kids had drawn pictures on top of their names. No wonder his back was so tired.

Lucy spun around. "You can use my back."

Lamont raised his eyebrows and grinned. "Snow Flake awaits you, Gordie."

"Hurry up and sign," snapped Lucy. "We're going to be late."

Gordie flipped the card over and signed

his name. He didn't draw a picture. He printed his name in small letters, leaving room for the rest of room nine to sign their names.

Gordie pushed the card under his sweater. Lucy took the pencil from him and snapped it in two.

"Hey, what are you doing, Lucy?" cried Gordie.

"What a Snow Flake thing to do," grumbled Lamont.

Lucy handed both Lamont and Gordie a pencil half. "It was an old, chewed-up pencil. Besides you're not letting me be the boss of this plan. So there!"

Gordie frowned as he watched Lucy race across the playground to get in line. He and Lamont started walking to the front door.

"She is one weird Snow Flake," said Lamont.

Gordie nodded. "She deserves a poisoned apple from the witch."

Lamont laughed as he started to run. "You're just saying that so you get to kiss her."

"Take that back, Lamont," said Gordie. He threw his pencil stub down on the ground.

"Got to catch me first, Prince."

Gordie tried to look mad, but started laughing as he ran after Lamont. He had almost caught up with him when Ms. Tingle stepped out of the line and stopped him.

"Hold on, Gordie."

Gordie looked up, puffing and trying to catch his breath.

"I'm afraid you broke two school rules in less than *five* seconds," said Ms. Tingle.

"What?" Gordie's eyes flew open as wide as they could. "Who told you?"

Ms. Tingle smiled. "We all saw you."

Gordie gulped. He thought he had been alone in the boys' restroom.

"You littered," said Ms. Tingle. She pointed behind Gordie.

Gordie saw the card lying on the playground.

"And you threw a pencil at Lamont," said Ms. Tingle. "Could you please go pick them up?"

"Come inside, class," said Ms. Tingle.

Gordie watched his class go up the stairs and disappear inside the double-glass doors. He took his time walking back across the playground. He picked up the card and put it back under his sweater. The pencil stub was in the middle of a puddle where it looked like some little kid had thrown up lunch.

Gordie kicked the pencil to get it out of the puddle. Then he kicked it over to the basketball hoop. A third kick sent the pencil flying up into the air. When it landed, it rolled slowly and then stopped. Gordie walked over and stared at it. One more kick would send it into the bushes where nobody would find it. Gordie drew his foot back, ready for the launch. Then he remembered that this was the first pencil

Ms. Tingle had ever given him, on the first day of third grade.

So even though the pencil had been in the barf puddle and had rolled over dirt and chewed gum, he bent down and picked it up. He wiped it off on his sweater and then put it into his pocket. Pretty soon it would be all he had left of Ms. Tingle.

Chapter

22

Gordie stopped at the water fountain and rinsed off his pencil stub. When he walked back into room nine, Lucy stuck out her tongue and then smiled. Gordie didn't smile back. One day someone would break *her* pencils and get *her* in trouble.

"Gordie? Are you okay?" asked Ms. Tingle.

"No, yes . . . I guess so." Gordie looked around. Even Lamont was staring at him with a worried look.

"You've been standing there for a few minutes. Do you want to sit down?" Ms. Tingle smiled. "You know I was only kidding about breaking school rules, right? I know you would never break school rules on purpose."

"Not on purpose," called out Lucy. "Sometimes, he—"

"Melt those lips, Snow Flake," said Lamont.

"Sit down, Gordie. Okay, class, we are almost ready to present our play to the school and our parents."

"Can we practice today, Ms. Tingle?" asked Lucy. "I don't even care if we can't wear our costumes. Please? Pretty, pretty with princess petals, please?"

"That's a good idea," said Mikey. "I think I know my lines, but then when we get onstage I forget most of them."

"Let's have rehearsal now," said Lucy. "We don't want to flop in front of the whole school, Ms. Tingle."

"They'll boo us," added Lamont.

Gordie stayed quiet in his seat. His back was tired from all the kids using him to sign the card, and his head was tired from being a sneaky kid. How did he end up feeling so bad in December when he started out so happy in September?

Suddenly the flashing lights made Gordie's head jerk up. Ms. Tingle was at the light switch, looking unhappy. Room nine got quiet.

"Settle down, class." She walked back to her desk and picked up her lesson-plan book. "We still have classroom work to finish."

"The play is next week," reminded Lamont. "Can we plow through the spelling, math, and reading, and get to the good stuff . . . like the play?"

Ms. Tingle smiled. "Sounds like a great idea, Lamont."

Gordie sat up taller in his seat. He felt like doing schoolwork now. That was the normal thing to do in third grade. Besides, it would keep his mind off the play, Ms. Tingle's wedding, and trying not to get kicked out of school.

For the next two hours, Gordie watched

room nine work as fast as they could. No one complained. No one tried to daydream or kick the seat of the kid in front of him. Ms. Tingle was so happy with the busy workers she canceled the spelling quiz.

"Good work, room nine. Let's rehearse." Ms. Tingle got out her script and then reached into her bottom drawer and pulled out a box of oatmeal cookies. "I made these myself, so let me know if I need to add more sugar or raisins. I really need to learn to bake well before Christmas."

Lucy jumped up from her desk. "I'll pass out the cookies, Ms. Tingle. I'm used to waiting on the seven dwarfs."

"Thank you, Lucy," said Ms. Tingle. "Okay, class, turn to the third act, scene two. This is where Lucy, I mean, Snow White, is sweeping the house and the witch gives her the apple."

Lucy handed the cookies to Lamont. "Here, Santa Lamont. Pass out the rest of the cookies because I've got sweeping to do."

Lamont bit into a cookie. "You're the

best baker, Ms. Tingle. Mr. Wilson is going to love these."

Ms. Tingle smiled. "I hope so because I have to make twenty dozen of them before Christmas. Okay, let's get the scripts and props and line up for a really fun rehearsal."

Gordie put his cookie inside his desk, next to the pencil stub. Now he had two souvenirs by which he could remember Ms. Tingle.

Everyone lined up. Ms. Tingle picked up a basket filled with more props for the play. "Lamont, do you have the bells? Mikey, get the elf hat from the radiator."

"We're all set, Ms. Tingle," called out Lucy. "I even have a little pillow so my head won't hurt when I fall asleep after eating the poisoned apple."

"Okay, okay." Ms. Tingle laughed. "If anyone else has a prop they want to use, bring it to the auditorium with you."

Lamont reached into his desk and pulled out a Santa Claus hat. Gordie had a crown that he had made out of aluminum foil. He hadn't wanted to wear it too early because it could get crushed if someone sat on it. But it was time now.

Ms. Tingle turned off the lights. "Line up, class."

As soon as she opened the door, Mr. Wilson walked in. Lamont elbowed Gordie. "Maybe Mr. Wilson wants to be in our play."

"He's Ms. Tingle's prince charming," whispered Lucy.

Ms. Tingle talked to Mr. Wilson and then smiled. "Class, Mr. Wilson and I have the most wonderful surprise for you."

"We already know," said Lucy.

Ms. Tingle looked confused. "You do?"

"Be quiet, Lucy," muttered Gordie.

Mr. Wilson took a step forward. "Let me tell them, Ms. Tingle."

"Here it comes," whispered Lamont. "Get ready to throw the rice, Gordie."

Gordie didn't smile. He was happy for Ms. Tingle because she was happy, but he wasn't a bit happy for himself.

"Ms. Tingle and I were talking this morning, and we decided room nine needed an audience for rehearsal. So I'm going to bring my fifth-grade computer class down to the auditorium to watch you."

"Yippee," cried Lucy. "Wait till you see how good I am, Mr. Wilson."

"Cool," added Mikey.

"Oh, no," groaned Gordie. His brother, Doug, was in the fifth grade. Lumpy Labriola was in the fifth grade.

"Sounds great," said Ms. Tingle. "We'll see you downstairs in a few minutes, Mr. Wilson."

"See you soon," said Mr. Wilson. "I hope you break a leg, kids."

"Break a leg?" muttered Gordie. Weren't things bad enough without Mr. Wilson hoping someone would fall off the stage and break a leg?

"*Break a leg* is a phrase actors use. It's a way to wish you all good luck," Ms. Tingle said.

Gordie followed Lamont out into the hall. Break a leg, break a leg, break a leg, thought Gordie. He kept chanting it all the way down the stairs to the auditorium. He needed all the good luck he could get.

Chapter 23

The moment Gordie walked into the auditorium, he got excited and nervous at the same time. Ms. Tingle led room nine up the stairs to the stage. She flicked on the yellow and blue lights and told everyone to study their lines for the last time.

Gordie and Lamont helped each other with their lines and then put their scripts on the floor. Ms. Tingle walked backstage, reminding everyone that the fifth-graders would be their first audience. Gordie and Lamont peeked out from behind the curtain as the fifth-graders walked into the auditorium.

"There's your brother, Gordie," whispered Lamont. "Will Doug clap for us?"

"Sure," said Gordie. "When I told him that I had to kiss Lucy's hand, he said it wasn't a big deal if I just pretended I was kissing my dog."

Lamont laughed. "Lucy probably has more fleas."

"I heard that, Lamont." Lucy shoved the boys aside and peered out at the audience. "There are about twenty kids out there. That's a pretty scrawny audience."

"At least we have one," said Gordie. "We won't be as nervous next Friday."

Lucy stepped back. "The only thing I'm nervous about is you forgetting your lines, Gordie."

Lamont leaned toward Lucy. "Why don't you go stuff your pillow in your mouth, Flaky."

Lucy pointed her finger at Gordie. "My big brothers will be really mad if you forget to kiss my hand, Gordie. You can't rewrite Snow White."

Lucy stomped off before Gordie could think of something smart-alecky to say back. Maybe he could ask Ms. Tingle to call the high school and tell them no one over twelve years old was allowed to watch the play, unless they were a parent.

"Boys, get backstage," said Ms. Tingle. "Good luck."

"Should we break a leg?" asked Lamont.

Ms. Tingle smiled. "Just try not to forget your lines."

Gordie and Lamont walked across the stage. Gordie thought the furniture made the stage look exactly like the home of the seven dwarfs. Lucy was already in place, holding a broom. Sneezy and Grumpy were seated at a small table that Ms. Tingle had borrowed from the kindergarten. The chairs were so small that Grumpy's knees touched his chin.

The auditorium lights were low, the stage lights brightened, and the curtain opened. Lamont jabbed Gordie in the back. "Good luck, buddy."

"Good luck," Gordie whispered back.

Chapter

24

Gordie's wish for good luck started when Lucy got the first big laugh from the audience. "Sneezy, you and Grumpy better get to the mines. The other five dwarfs are waiting. I'm tired of waiting to be rescued. I don't like sweeping and cooking." Lucy started sweeping faster and faster. "I wish this broom were magic so I could fly out of here. I just know I should be a princess and not a housekeeper."

Gordie watched Ms. Tingle smile when she heard the laughter. Then she pushed two elves out onto the stage. She pointed to Lamont and then the stage.

"Here I go," muttered Lamont. He pulled his hat down and smiled.

Gordie couldn't believe how much funnier the play seemed with an audience laughing. Everyone was doing a great job.

Ms. Tingle tiptoed over and put her hand on Gordie's shoulder. "As soon as Lucy takes the apple from Leslie, get ready. Once she falls down you go in. Kiss her hand, and it's all over."

Gordie nodded. He only had a few lines. He could do it. He'd do it for Ms. Tingle.

Gordie looked past the stage and out into the audience. Mr. Wilson was sitting next to Lumpy. Lumpy was frowning, so he must have gotten yelled at. The rest of the fifth-graders were laughing. Doug was sitting in the front row.

Onstage Lamont and the elves were leaving with Grumpy and Sneezy. They exited, and Lamont waved to Gordie from the other side.

Leslie knocked on the fake door and walked in. "Hello. I am an old lady who is lost in the forest. I came to cut down a Christmas tree."

"Oh, my," said Lucy. "I'm Snow White. I am a princess who was dropped off in the forest. One day I will find my way back home. I am tired of doing so much laundry for the dwarfs. They get awful dirty in the mine. Their socks stink."

The fifth-graders laughed, even Lumpy. Gordie was getting excited to go onstage now. He hoped he could make the fifth-graders laugh, especially Lumpy.

"I am thirsty, Snow White," said Leslie. "May I have a sip of water?"

Lucy hurried over to a red bucket and dipped in the ladle. "Of course you can, Old Woman. Snow White is not only beautiful, but kind."

Gordie frowned. Lucy made that line up. He glanced over at Ms. Tingle. She was smiling. Gordie smiled, too. It must be okay to make up lines if you were onstage.

Lucy twirled around twice and then gave the old woman the water.

"You are very kind," said Leslie. "I want to give you a present."

"I love presents," said Lucy. She twirled around again, even though she wasn't supposed to. "What are you going to give me?"

Gordie stood up straighter. It was almost his turn to go onstage. He drew in a deep breath. Break a leg, break a leg, break a leg, he chanted to himself.

"I said, 'What are you going to give me,' Old Woman?" Lucy asked again.

Gordie looked over at Leslie, who looked as if she was going to cry.

Lucy stepped closer to Leslie. "I gave you some water so you have to give me something, Leslie, I mean, Old Woman."

A few fifth-graders laughed. Lumpy let out a quick boo.

Gordie looked over at Ms. Tingle, who was searching behind the stage curtain with a flashlight.

"I want to give you something," stammered Leslie. "I really do."

"Then give it to me," snapped Lucy. Her face was getting very red.

Leslie pulled off her watch and handed it to Lucy. "Here, take this."

Lucy stared at the watch. "I don't want a watch."

Lots of kids were laughing.

Gordie bit his lip. What was Leslie doing? Why didn't she just give Lucy the apple? Was she making up lines, too?

Ms. Tingle hurried over to Gordie. "Where's the apple? Leslie needs the apple."

Gordie had never seen Ms. Tingle look so worried, not even when Mr. Wilson handed her the envelope.

"Lucy doesn't know what to do," whispered Ms. Tingle.

Gordie bent down, lifting scripts from the backstage floor. "I hope she doesn't run off the stage." If Lucy ran off the stage, he wouldn't have to kiss her. But it would ruin Ms. Tingle's play.

"I know you want to give me something," said Lucy. "I'm hungry. Do you have any food on you, Old Woman?"

"No, I don't know where my food is," said Leslie.

"Well, you better find it fast, lady," snapped Lucy.

Gordie lifted one of the elves' shoes and saw the apple.

"Here it is," he whispered.

"What are we going to do?" asked Ms. Tingle. "Lucy is upset."

Gordie knew that Lucy got upset a lot, but never in front of a room filled with fifth-graders.

"I'll sneak over and give Leslie the apple," whispered Gordie. "It will be okay."

Ms. Tingle smiled and nodded. Gordie walked quickly, trying to be careful not to bump the curtain. He was almost there when Leslie started to cry.

"I don't have food, but maybe I can find something here to give you," said Leslie. "Do you want some tea?"

"Are you nuts?" cried Lucy. "You're

supposed to give me something right now." Lucy ran her fingers through her hair. "I don't believe this, Leslie, I mean, Old Woman."

More kids started to laugh. Gordie stared down at the apple. From the fake door he could see Lucy biting every fingernail she had.

Gordie hurried through the door.

"What are you doing here?" asked Lucy. Her hair was sticking up like she was in the middle of a windstorm.

More and more fifth-graders laughed. Mr. Wilson was laughing, too. Everyone was laughing except Ms. Tingle and room nine.

"My name is Prince. . . ." Gordie couldn't remember if he had a name. "Prince . . . Lamont. I heard that a nice lady named Snow Flake, I mean, Snow White, lived here."

Lucy was staring at Gordie like he had three heads. "I'm Snow White."

Gordie shoved the apple toward Lucy.

"Well, I found this apple outside, and I thought it might be yours."

Leslie snatched the apple. "I must have dropped it." She turned and handed Lucy the apple. "Here, this is what I wanted to give you. Can I have my watch back? My mom will be mad if I lose it."

Lucy frowned and handed the watch to Leslie. "Thank you, Old Woman. Now you better leave because I have to wash out some socks for the seven dwarfs."

"Fine," snapped Leslie. "It's not my fault I couldn't find the apple." Leslie stomped off the stage, not even leaving through the fake door.

Gordie and Lucy stared at each other. Gordie couldn't say his real first line, "Awaken, fair maiden," because Lucy was standing right there, wide-awake, holding the apple.

Lucy sighed. "Well, I better go wash this apple."

Gordie nodded. "Okay. I think I better go ride my horse."

"Okay," said Lucy. She still looked worried.

"So you just wash that apple," said Gordie. "Good-bye and farewell."

"Farewell," said Lucy.

Ms. Tingle was waiting for Gordie when he walked off the stage. She gave him a big thumbs-up sign. Gordie turned around and watched Lucy walking around the stage. Gordie sighed, still nervous. He and Lucy were making up their own lines so much he wasn't sure he remembered the *real* ones Ms. Tingle had written.

Lucy dipped the apple into the bucket. "I am so hungry that I am going to take a bite of this apple." Lucy took a bite and then twirled around two times. "Oh, my. I feel terrible. I feel so—" Lucy gave one last, slow spin and slumped to the floor, resting her head on the small pillow.

Ms. Tingle nodded at Gordie.

"Hello, hello?" called Gordie as he walked through the fake door. "Is anybody home?"

Gordie walked closer. Lucy's hair was sticking up so much you couldn't even see the pillow. She didn't look like Snow White at all. She looked like a worn-out Lucy Diaz.

"Oh, what happened here?" asked Gordie. He bent down and picked up the apple. "I bet this apple is filled with poison."

A few kids laughed, even though this was supposed to be the sad part of the play. Gordie knew he could make the fifth-graders laugh if he made up a line like,

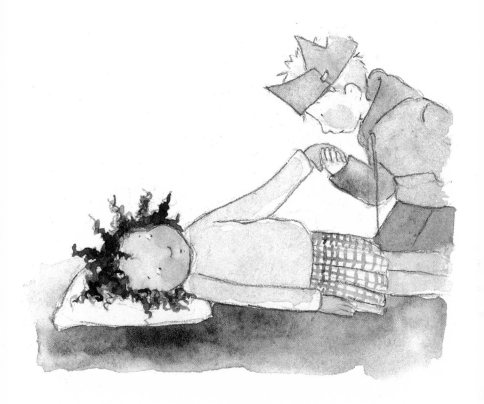

"Good, Snow Flake is dead." But that wasn't in the play that Ms. Tingle had written.

"I wonder if a . . . a kiss would awaken this maiden," said Gordie.

There was a lot of laughter, but then lots of shushing noises.

Gordie bent down and lifted Lucy's hand. It was hot and sweaty, not like Gordie's dog's cool paw at all.

"Awaken, fair maiden," said Gordie. He kissed her hand, then stood up.

No one laughed. Not even Lumpy Labriola.

Lucy stretched and stood up. She smiled at Gordie. It was a big smile, like she was smiling at a real prince.

"Thank you," she said.

"You're welcome," said Gordie. "You better throw that apple away before the seven dwarfs and Santa get back."

"I will." Lucy took the apple and put it into the trash. "Well, farewell, Prince Lamont. Thanks for everything."

Gordie smiled. Lucy had made up the thank-you line.

"I must return to my castle in New London," said Gordie.

Lucy ran up to Gordie. "New London? That is next to my kingdom, Old London."

"You're kidding," said Gordie. "You can ride on my horse with me if you want to go home."

Lucy twirled around and around. "I'll be home for the holidays!"

"Will the seven dwarfs miss you?" asked Gordie. "Who will cook and clean and wash out their socks?"

"Let Santa and his elves do it. They will all be just fine." Lucy twirled over to the coatrack and took her red cape. It was the same cape she had worn for Halloween when she was Little Red Riding Hood.

"Let's get on the horse," said Gordie. "We'll all be home for Christmas." Gordie held out his arm like he'd seen a movie star do in an old movie. Lucy grabbed on, and they both squeezed through the fake door. It only tore a little.

The audience started clapping before the curtain even closed. Once it was closed, room nine hurried out and stood in a straight line behind the curtain.

"Remember to smile and bow," called out Ms. Tingle from the wings. She pulled on the curtain ropes, and the curtain opened.

The audience clapped and whistled.

Gordie bowed with the rest of the class. The fifth-graders kept clapping. Gordie wasn't sure if the play was that good or if the fifth-graders were just glad to be out of computer class.

Ms. Tingle walked out onstage, and the fifth-graders clapped harder. Mr. Wilson stood up, holding a long red rose.

Gordie and Lamont looked at each other. Was Mr. Wilson going to announce he was going to marry Ms. Tingle in front of everyone?

Mr. Wilson walked up the side stairs and handed Ms. Tingle the rose.

"Wonderful, wonderful," said Mr. Wilson. "Really wonderful."

Ms. Tingle took the rose. "Thank you so much."

Mr. Wilson held up both hands, and the clapping finally stopped. "I think the third-graders did a great job with the play. And I am very proud of the fifth-graders for being such a good, polite audience."

Gordie waited for Mr. Wilson to pull out a ring. He waited for him to get down on one knee, but Mr. Wilson just walked back down the side stairs and told Lumpy to stop fooling around.

Once the curtain closed, Ms. Tingle clapped her hands. "You are such good actors and actresses. We had a small problem with the apple, but it worked out so well." Ms. Tingle laughed. "In fact, I think some of your own lines were funnier than mine. I may rewrite the play for next year."

Gordie looked down at the floor. Next month kids in Ohio would be having fun with Ms. Tingle, and Gordie in room nine would miss her. He'd miss her a lot.

"Can we take a field trip to Ohio and watch it?" asked Lamont.

"Ohio?" Ms. Tingle shook her head. "Why Ohio?"

Gordie looked up. She had to tell them the truth now.

"Aren't you going to move to Ohio with Mr. Wilson?" asked Lucy. "You know, after you get married this Christmas."

Ms. Tingle was silent, then she laughed. She laughed so hard she had to wipe the tears from the corners of her eyes.

Gordie didn't think that Ms. Tingle's getting married was funny.

"I'm not going to marry Mr. Wilson," she finally said.

"But Lucy saw you eating spaghetti with Mr. Wilson," Gordie said quickly. "He wiped sauce off your face."

"And he gives you doughnuts and secret envelopes," added Lamont.

Ms. Tingle laughed again. "Some of you are too busy minding *my* business."

"We don't want you to go," said Gordie. "Please stay with us!"

Ms. Tingle smiled. "Oh, children, thank you. I'm not leaving room nine. I've been helping Mr. Wilson plan his wedding to my cousin Laura Tingle. Mr. Wilson discovered that the rehearsal hall has a huge leak in the ceiling, so we're trying to reorganize.

But things will all turn out fine. You guys are stuck with me for the rest of the year."

Gordie was the first one to clap, then Lucy, Lamont, Mikey, Leslie, and the rest of room nine. They clapped harder than the whole fifth-grade audience.

As Gordie was busy clapping, he felt his stomach itch. He couldn't figure out why—he wasn't nervous anymore, not since he had kissed Lucy's sweaty hand. Then he scratched his stomach and felt Ms. Tingle's card.

"Wait, Ms. Tingle," he shouted. "Room nine has a surprise for you."

Lucy groaned. "It better be a good surprise."

"It is," said Lamont. He elbowed Gordie. "Give it to Ms. Tingle, your Royal Highness."

Gordie smiled as he handed Ms. Tingle the card. "We all signed it because you are a wonderful writer. And a very nice teacher."

Ms. Tingle opened the card. "Thank you, everyone." She smiled at them all and then looked right at Gordie. "And you are a true prince."

"Thank you," Gordie whispered back. He felt like one.